D1053249

Frog and Friends

Outdoor Surprises

Written by Eve Bunting

Illustrated by Josée Masse

To Anna Eve Bunting

—*Eve*

For my sister Brigitte and my niece Audrey

—*Josée*

This book has a reading comprehension level of 2.3 under the ATOS® readability formula.
For information about ATOS please visit www.renlearn.com.
ATOS is a registered trademark of Renaissance Learning, Inc.

Lexile®, Lexile® Framework and the Lexile® logo are trademarks of MetaMetrics, Inc.,
and are registered in the United States and abroad. The trademarks and names of other
companies and products mentioned herein are the property of their respective owners.
Copyright © 2010 MetaMetrics, Inc. All rights reserved.

Sleeping Bear Press™

315 E. Eisenhower Parkway, Ste. 200
Ann Arbor, MI 48108
www.sleepingbearpress.com

Printed and bound in the United States.

10 9 8 7 6 5 4 3 2 1

Library of Congress Cataloging-in-Publication Data • Bunting, Eve, 1928- • Frog and friends : outdoor surprises / written by Eve Bunting; • illustrated by Josée Masse. • v. cm. • Summary: "A beginning reader book containing three stories featuring Frog and his friends where Frog joins a singing group, helps rescue a baby bird, and is scared by a nighttime story"–Provided by publisher. • Contents: Frog and the Pond Singers — Frog and the baby bird — A big scary story. • ISBN 978-1-58536-807-5 (hard cover) — ISBN 978-1-58536-808-2 (paper back) • [1. Frogs–Fiction. 2. Animals–Fiction. 3. Friendship–Fiction. 4. Ponds–Fiction.] I. Masse, Josée, ill. II. Title. III. Title: Outdoor surprises. • PZ7. B91527Fsm 2013 • [E]–dc23 • 2012040718

Table of Contents

Frog and the Pond Singers

One day Frog told Raccoon, "We should

have a singing concert."

"Great idea," Raccoon said. "We know a lot of good songs."

Raccoon and Possum and Rabbit and Squirrel and Chameleon and little Jumping Mouse liked the idea, too.

"We will tell everyone!"

They scratched out signs on the ground

that pointed toward the pond.

CONCERT AT THE POND
AT SUNSET
THE DAY AFTER THE DAY AFTER
THE DAY AFTER TOMORROW.

They asked the birds to help spread the

word.

Frog asked the crickets to sing with them. They practiced and practiced.

Squeal, squeak, chirp, croak, yelp, peep, and harrumph dee-dee.

Their voices went well together.

On the night before the concert Frog was excited.

He was also worried. His throat was sore.

He gargled with pond water.

He knew honey was good for sore throats. He ate two honeybees.

He asked Raccoon to tie his pretty blue scarf around where his neck would be. If he had a neck.

Chameleon brought him hot soup with four fat flies in it.

"Chicken soup is good for colds," he said. "Fly soup is better for sore throats."

Nothing helped.

The next day Frog tried to sing.

His harrumph dee-dee had vanished.

So sad!

At sunset there was a crowd.

The Pond Singers were ready.

Frog hung his head. "I cannot sing," he told them. "My throat is too sore."

Possum stroked his back. "Do not be sad," she said. "Come and stand with us anyway."

There was a clapping of paws and a
stomping of feet from the crowd.

The Pond Singers started to sing.

"WE WANT FROG!" the crowd
yelled. **"SING, FROG, SING!"**

Frog croaked as loud as he could, "I
cannot sing … I have a frog in my throat!"

The crowd clapped. "Funny! Funny!"

Frog smiled.

"I can still play baseball," he croaked.

"I like baseball, I like to catch pop flies."

He stuck out his long, sticky tongue.

The crowd shouted, "Funny! Funny!"

Frog smiled again. This was good.

When the concert was over Possum stepped up. "The singers were Raccoon, Squirrel, Chameleon, Rabbit, little Jumping Mouse, the Fearless Crickets, and me, Possum."

The singers bowed.

"And …" Possum said, "the jokes were by Frog."

There was more cheering.

Frog bowed too.

He had been a part of it after all.

And that made him very HOPPY!

Frog and the Baby Bird

One day there was a big wind.

The water in Frog's pond made little

waves. It was fun to jump through them.

Frog was happy to think of Raccoon

and Possum and Rabbit and Chameleon

and Squirrel and little Jumping Mouse safe

and snug in their homes.

He looked around.

There were tree branches on the

ground. And lots of leaves. But there was

something else.

Frog hopped out of his pond.

He went to see what the something else was.

It was a bird's nest.

And there was a baby bird inside it.

Oh no, Frog thought. The nest has

blown down from the tree.

"Do not worry, baby bird," he croaked.

"We will take care of you."

Frog showed his friends the baby bird.

"It needs its mother," Possum said.

"It needs to be warm," Raccoon said.

"I could bundle it in my pretty blue

scarf," Frog said.

Just then a robin flew down from the
tree.

She flew around the nest. She was crying,
"My baby, my baby!"

Frog was so sorry for the mother bird.

Then he had an idea.

"Squirrel," Frog said, "you could climb
the tree. You could take the nest back up."

"Oh my!" Squirrel said. "I need all my
paws to climb. I might fall."

"Please, *please*," the mother bird

begged. "Some other animal may come

along. It may not be as kind as you are.

My baby needs to be safe in the tree."

Squirrel scratched his head. "Oh, all

right. I will try."

"Thank you! Thank you, Squirrel." The mother bird swooped over. She kissed Squirrel's head.

Squirrel picked up the nest.

"Careful! Careful!" the mother bird cried. "Do not drop it."

"**Humph!**" Squirrel said. "I will try to not drop the nest. And I will try to not drop me."

He began to climb.

Frog and Possum and her little ones and Raccoon and Rabbit and Chameleon and little Jumping Mouse stood under the tree.

UP, UP, UP Squirrel went.

"We will catch you if you fall!" Frog shouted.

Possum sent her little possums away. "If Squirrel falls on you he will squash you," she told them. **"Shoo! Shoo!"**

The mother bird twittered around
Squirrel's head.

"Do not drop my baby," she chirped.
"Be careful."

"Do not bother me," Squirrel said.
"Where shall I put the nest?"

"Here." Mama Bird showed him a branch.

Squirrel set the nest down carefully.

"Phew!" he muttered.

"Hurrah! Hurrah! Well done!" his friends called up.

"Thank you, Squirrel," Mama Bird said. She snuggled in the nest, close to her baby.

Squirrel felt good.

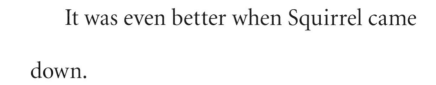

It was even better when Squirrel came down.

His friends rushed to clap him on the back.

"You are our hero," they told him.

"It was Frog's idea," Squirrel said.

Frog smiled.

That was true.

He often had good ideas.

Frog and the Big Scary Story

It was midnight. Frog and his friends

sat around the pond.

"Will you tell us a story, little Jumping Mouse?" Squirrel asked.

"It is midnight. So I will tell you a *scary* story," little Jumping Mouse said.

It was dark. There was a half moon. There were lots of shadows.

"Once upon a time," little Jumping Mouse began.

"That is how all good stories start," Possum told the others.

"Once upon a time there were seven friends," little Jumping Mouse said.

"Like us," Frog agreed.

"But we also have my little possums," Possum reminded them.

"That is true."

"The seven friends sat around a pond."

"Like us," Rabbit said.

"Suddenly there was a big, Big, BIG noise." Little Jumping Mouse went on, "It came from out of the dark."

Frog shivered. "Ooooh, creepy!"

"The big, Big, BIG noise came closer,"
little Jumping Mouse said. Her voice was
creepy now, too. "Closer and closer and
closer."

Possum peered into the dark around
them.

"Then a big giant something came out of the shadows," little Jumping Mouse said. **"OH, OH, OH!"** Raccoon howled. "I am getting too scared!"

"I *hear* the BIG SCARY SOMETHING!" Squirrel said. "He is under the trees! He is coming!"

"You only *think* you hear him," Frog said, but he was shaking. He told himself it was just because it was cold out of the water.

There was a thumping sound.

Chameleon made himself brown, the color of the dirt. "That way the BIG SCARY SOMETHING will not see me!" he said.

Possum put her paws over the eyes of her little ones.

A big, scary black shadow stood in the
grass.

"Run!" Frog yelled. "Jump! Scamper!
Hop! Climb a tree! It is the BIG SCARY
SOMETHING!!"

Suddenly a big, BIG voice said, "Do not run. I came out for a night walk. I heard the storyteller. I love stories. May I sit with you?"

Frog gave a happy hop.

"It is only Hippo," he told the others. "You know him. He is our friend from the Little Zoo. He can come out of the zoo any time he wants to."

40

"I was not scared," Raccoon told Hippo.

"You were, too," Squirrel said. "You

howled."

"I think I do not like scary stories,"

Chameleon said.

"Where are you?" Squirrel asked.

"Over here. Hiding in the dirt,"

Chameleon said.

Rabbit fanned herself with a leaf.

"Will you tell us a *not*-scary story, Jumping Mouse?" she asked.

"Oh, please." Hippo sat down beside them.

"I will tell you a story about a cow who jumped over the moon," little Jumping Mouse said.

They sat together, listening. It was a good story.

"I like a story with a HOPPY ending like that," Rabbit said.

They were not scared anymore.

They lay down together to sleep.

Frog curled up next to big Hippo.

It was nice to have a big, big friend to

sleep over with.

After a scary story.